Where Dani goes, happy follows

Rose Lagercrantz

Eva Eriksson

GECKO PRESS

CONTENTS

Part 1

Chapter 1 7

Chapter 2 17

Chapter 3 21

Chapter 4 27

Chapter 5 33

Chapter 6 39

Chapter 7 47

Chapter 8 55

Chapter 9 61

Chapter 10 69

Part 2

Chapter 11 79

Chapter 12 85

Chapter 13 93

Chapter 14 97

Chapter 15 105

Chapter 16 111

Chapter 17 121

Chapter 18 131

Part 3

Chapter 19 139

Chapter 20 145

Chapter 21 151

Chapter 22 157

Part 4

Chapter 23 165

Chapter 24 173

Chapter 25 177

1

Chapter 1

Here is some more about Dani, the girl who lives in the yellow house on Home Street with her father, and with Cat and her two hamsters.

"Happy Dani," as her teacher calls her.

One of her happiest things every day is going to school.

The best thing about school is her teacher. Dani loves her. She also loves science. And art and silent reading. And her friends.

The best part of school is practically all of it. At school she is like a fish in water. She is in the place she feels happy.

That spring term in year two, everyone in Dani's class was like a fish in water. Especially Cushion, but he feels happy wherever he is, whatever happens.

When their teacher asked them to talk about something they'd done during the break that was fun, he put his hand up straight away and said:

"When I was bitten by a dog."

Everyone fell silent. What did he say?

The teacher came and looked at him carefully.

"Did I hear right?" she asked. "When you were bitten by a dog? Was that really *fun*?"

"Not the actual bite," Cushion admitted, "and not the tetanus injection either, of course."

"Did you get stitches?" Vicky interrupted.

"You don't get stitches for dog bites," explained Cushion. "You get something to cover the wound."

"How many holes were there?" Jonathan wondered.

They had so many questions that Cushion lost track.

"What's the fun part?" Benny complained.

"Will you be quiet so Cushion can go on!" said Dani.

Cushion gave her a grateful look and paused.

Everyone waited.

"Then my father said I could have my own dog!"

A shiver went through the class.

"We've already been to look at her," Cushion went on. "Her name's Dina and she's never bitten anyone!"

"Well, I can understand that was fun," the teacher admitted.

And then it was time for art. Everyone drew dogs biting people, except for Dani, who drew a squirrel. And Cushion, who wandered around the class admiring everyone's drawings.

When he came to Dani's desk, he just stood and watched.

"Nice!" he said at last.

"Ugh," Dani mumbled.

Cushion looked longingly at the empty place beside her, the one where Dani's best friend Ella sat before she had to move to Northbrook.

The desk had been empty for a whole year. No one's allowed to sit there, because Dani still believes that Ella will come back to the class.

Cushion no longer asks to sit there even though he wants to. He loves Dani so much.

For Cushion, Dani is the best thing about school.

What about Dani though? Does she love Cushion?

Maybe, maybe not. She hasn't had much to compare with.

She's only been in love once before. That was when she was little and went to day care.

There was a boy called Max...

They played together every day, behind a big rock.
But one day he called Dani Poo-head.

"When Grandma heard that she was angry.

"Maybe he forgot my name," Dani defended him.
"Max can be a bit forgetful."

"If he says it again, you must tell him that your
name is Daniela," said Grandma.

But she didn't need to. They didn't play together
again after that.

That happened when Dani was living with her
grandma and grandpa, because her mother had died.
Her father was so sad that he couldn't look after her.

It was only when Dani started school that he felt
well enough for her to move back home to live with
him and Cat.

Chapter 2

But when Dani was in year two at school, it happened again!

Just as the winter break was about to start, Dani's father got sad again. He felt so awful he had to go away for a while to think about other things.

He thought it would do him good to go to Rome, the city where he was born, and talk with his mother, Lucia, and his brother, Giuseppe.

And Giuseppe's wife, Donatella. And their children, Rosanna and Alessandro.

Dani wanted to go too. It was years since she'd seen her Italian family.

But that wasn't to be. Her father had decided to go on his own. He needed to think about his life.

"It's not good for you to be with someone so sad!" he said.

"Can't you say why you're that way?" Dani tried.

But he didn't want to talk about it.

Instead of going to Rome, Dani went to live with Grandma and Grandpa again.

This break wouldn't be much fun, she thought, when Grandma came to get her and the hamsters. The people next door had promised to look after Cat.

Dani left Home Street with a heavy heart.

But Grandma was thrilled! Having Dani in the house was the best thing she could think of.

Chapter 3

Cushion wasn't happy either about the break from school.

A whole week without Dani!

How could he bear it?

As soon as he got up on the first morning, he started to think. And soon he had an idea.

He'd go over to Dani's house with a little surprise…

When the flower shop opened, Cushion was there waiting to buy Dani a flower, a red rose. The most beautiful one they had.

It was expensive, but he'd been given some money
by his grandmother, so he had enough.

Then he hurried to the yellow house on Home Street and rang the doorbell.

To his disappointment it wasn't Dani who came to the door, but her father, Gianni.

"Is Dani awake yet?" Cushion asked.

"I'm sorry," said her father. "Dani's with her grandma and grandpa."

Cushion peered into the hallway, as if he didn't think he'd heard properly.

"I'm in a bit of a hurry, on my way to the airport," Gianni said impatiently.

"Without Dani?"

"Yes, unfortunately. This time. I'm not feeling well and need to talk with my mother. See you later, Cushion!"

But Cushion stood there, thinking to himself.

What should he do with the rose?

"I was going to give her
this." He held out the rose.

Dani's father gave it a
bewildered look.

"She'd love that!" he said.

"But she won't be home before it's wilted."

"I can take it to her," Cushion suggested. "Can you give me the address?"

"What address?"

"Of her grandma and grandpa."

"Are you thinking you'll take the train?"

"No, my dad will drive me."

Gianni went into the hallway and wrote on a piece of paper.

"They live on the other side of town," he explained. "Quite far away."

"Yeah, okay," muttered Cushion, and he took the piece of paper and went on his way.

Chapter 4

Over on the other side of town, Dani was lying in bed in her mother's old bedroom with the bedcovers up to her nose, thinking: no school for a whole week!

What could she do?

There was a knock at the door and Grandma and Grandpa peeped in.

"Are you awake, Dani?"

"Yes," Dani sighed and sat up.

"Up with the corners of your mouth," said Grandpa. "Look what I've found in the basement!"

He held up a pair of skis in one hand and a pair of boots in the other—cousin Sven's old ones.

And Grandma waved the poles, and a headband like the ones the Olympic skiers wear.

Dani perked up and decided to begin the day with a ski tour.

It might be quite nice. It had been snowing for days and nights. And now the snow had settled, and everything was white. The day before she'd seen some fresh ski tracks outside the house.

She hopped out of bed, put on her clothes, ate a sandwich and drank a little tea.

Then she was ready to start the new day.

Grandpa helped her put on her skis.

And then off she went. Gosh, she was going fast!

She could ski almost like a professional, she thought.

"I didn't know I was so good at cross-country skiing," she muttered, and she went a bit faster.

After a while she came to a stop and looked tentatively up at a small hill.

Would she be able to climb that?

She took a deep breath and made a start.

Everything went pretty well.

Up, up, up, till she reached the top.

Chapter 5

While Dani was climbing the small hill, her father called from the airport. He wanted to tell her that he was already feeling a little better.

"Yes, it's remarkable how a trip away can pick you up," said Grandpa.

"But I should have brought my *principessa* with me!" Gianni went on.

Principessa is Italian and means *princess*. That's what he calls Dani, sometimes, when he doesn't call her *Amore*.

"Is she missing me terribly?"

"Don't worry about her," said Grandpa. "The *principessa* is out having fun on the cross-country trail."

"Bravo!" said Gianni. "Tell her that a boy called in this morning with a flower for her."

"What boy?"

"A cute boy with dark curly hair."

"Well, I'll be blowed! I'll tell her," Grandpa promised.

He opened the window and called out to Dani, but she was too far away to hear.

She was standing on top of the hill, getting herself ready to ski down it.

"Watch out below!" she called and away she went.

I didn't know I was so good at downhill skiing, she was thinking, just before she lost her balance…

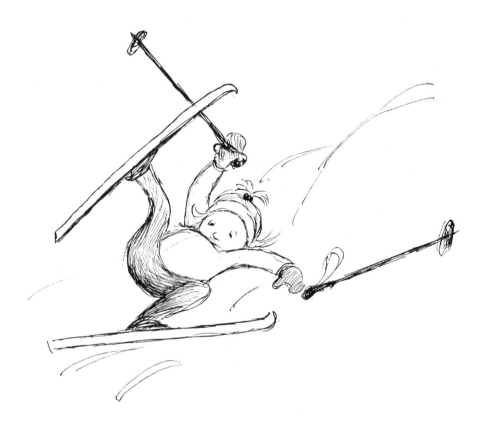

…and ended up in a snowdrift.
She lay there laughing to herself.

36

"Happy comes and happy goes…" she murmured as she crossed her skis in the air.

That's the beginning of a poem her mother used to read to her, so Grandma says.

But how did the rest of it go? She'd like to know.

Suddenly she was gloomy again.

Not so strange, perhaps, when you have a father on his way to Rome without his daughter, even though it was the winter break.

But if Dani could choose, there was one place she'd like to go to even more. Most of all she wanted to go to Northbrook to see her best friend in the whole world.

"Ella," she said to herself. "Can you hear me?"

She did that sometimes, talking to herself. To Ella.

"It's been so long!" she continued. "But I'll think up some way we can see each other again…"

Chapter 6

Ella is a whole chapter in Dani's life.

Dani is never happier than when they can be together, ideally day and night, without having to leave each other's sight for a single minute. Only when one of them has to go to the bathroom.

But even then, Ella tries to hold on till it's almost too late.

One time when she'd been hopping around with her legs crossed, her mother told her to go to the bathroom before an accident happened.

But Ella didn't have time.

That was the time they'd pulled a whole lot of books from the shelves and played librarians.

They made library cards and they lent books and borrowed them back and paid all their fines.

It might not sound very special, but it was. Everything is special with Ella.

"I haven't got time to pee!" she yelled at her mother.

"You do have time! Now do as I say!" her mother ordered.

"You can't tell me what to do!" shrieked Ella.

"Yes, I can!" said her mother. "Until you're eighteen. Then you can decide for yourself."

"When I'm eighteen I'll never stop to pee!" Ella shrieked and she rushed into the bathroom and was away for at least two minutes.

But that was a long time ago. Now they hadn't played together for ages.

Every time Dani complains to her father that she can't see Ella, he says it's a shame but it can't be helped.

"You have to learn to put things behind you and move on," he'd say.

"But hello there," Dani protested the last time he said it. "Ella is not a *thing*!"

That stopped him.

"I'm sorry," he mumbled, and looked ashamed. "I do know how that feels…"

But what good came of that?

If Dani and Ella want to see each other, they have to arrange it themselves.

That's how it is now.

Suddenly Dani had an idea as she lay there in the snow, a real lightning strike! She sat up.

Ella's birthday was coming up…

That was it! It was at the start of the winter break. Ella had reminded her about it last time they spoke on the phone.

Eagerly Dani blinked away a snowflake that had landed on one eyelid.

She had thought up the world's best birthday present!

Quickly she got to her feet and skied back to Grandma and Grandpa's house.

She took off her skis, rushed up the steps and put her thumb on the doorbell. She didn't take it off until Grandma opened the door.

"Could someone drive me to Northbrook?" she puffed.

Grandma looked at her in surprise.

"It's Ella's birthday!" Dani explained.

She lifted her nose and sniffed the air. What was smelling so good?

"Help, my jam cakes!" cried Grandma and she ran back to the kitchen.

Chapter 7

The little cakes were perfectly done. Grandma took out the tray and got ready to listen.

"Tell me again what you said?" she asked.

"It's Ella's birthday," Dani said again. "And I've thought up the world's best birthday present."

"What could that be?"

"An event!"

"A *what?*"

"An experience. Not a thing, but something you can *do.* That's what people give each other nowadays. They go to the movies or the amusement park.

Dani wormed her finger into the pie that was cooling on the table.

Grandma pretended not to see.

"And what are you planning to give Ella for an experience, then?" she wanted to know.

"You'll never guess," Dani said mysteriously.

"No, I probably won't," agreed Grandma.

"Me!" said Dani. "Suddenly, there I am! Do you get it?"

"No, not exactly."

"Like this…"

She pulled off her headband, took Grandma's blue felt pen from the kitchen drawer and wrote on the band in great big letters, before she put it back on again.

"Best present," Grandma read.

"Now do you get it?" asked Dani.

"Yes, I'm beginning to get the idea," said Grandma. "The experience is that you…"

"Exactly!" said Dani, beaming. "That I go to Northbrook!"

"And how do you imagine that will happen?"

"Ohhh," said Dani, "you are so slow today! You'll drive me there, of course."

Grandma looked blankly at her.

"That's not possible, my love. As you can see, I'm in the middle of preparing for my bridge friends' annual dinner."

"Then Grandpa will drive me!" said Dani.

That wasn't possible either.

"Grandpa has just taken the car in to be serviced," Grandma explained.

Dani looked at her in dismay.

Grandma began to remove the jam cakes from the tray.

"And I'm not sure that your father would give the green light for that."

"What do you mean, the green light?"

"That's what you say when you allow something."

"Do you think the same as him?" asked Dani. "Do you also think Ella and I should forget each other?"

Grandma looked up.

"Has he said that? I can't believe he would!"

"He always says that," said Dani.

"That is the silliest thing I've heard." Grandma tried to shake out the last cakes. "Of course you and Ella should get together. Especially on your birthdays. We'll just have to work out how."

She thought for a moment. Then she looked long and searchingly at Dani.

"Do you think you'd dare to go there on your own?" she asked.

Dani's eyes went as round as buttons.

"Would you dare go on your own if I put you on a train in Stockholm and Ella's mother collected you from the station in Northbrook?"

Dani swallowed.

"Of course I would," she said.

"Then I'll see what Sonja thinks," said Grandma,
and she went out to make a call.

Sonja, that's Ella's mother.

"There. It's all arranged," she said when she'd finished talking. "Sonja thinks it's an excellent idea for you to come. She'll meet you at the station at five minutes to two. Paddy and Ella's little sister will be there as well. How about that! A whole welcoming committee!"

It sounded too good to be true!

"But," said Dani, "she won't say anything to Ella, will she?"

"Of course not. Ella will be at her riding school. Is that good?"

"Perfect!"

Now they just needed to convince Grandpa too.

That wouldn't be so easy.

Chapter 8

And nor was it.

When Grandpa came home from the mechanic and heard what was planned, he shook his head.

"Have you lost your mind?" he asked Grandma. "You don't let a small girl travel alone from Stockholm all the way to Northbrook!"

Grandma hesitated for a second.

"What could happen, really?" she asked, crossing her arms.

"Quite a lot," said Grandpa. "Practically anything! Do you not read the newspaper any more?"

"No," said Grandma. "Then
one wouldn't dare do anything!"
   She took a step closer and
lowered her voice so that Dani
couldn't hear.

But Dani has fantastic hearing!

"I can't bear to see Dani all alone for the whole break," she heard Grandma explain. "And Sven got to go skiing with a friend. Do you think that's fair?"

It was just the right question. It went straight to Grandpa's heart.

Grandpa liked everything to be fair. His grandchildren should have everything *exactly* the same. They should have the same number of presents, for example, and if Sven went away on a trip then Dani should also be allowed to.

He thought for a moment.

"Gianni will have to decide," he said.

Grandma took the phone again and called Dani's father's number. Then she put it on speakerphone so Grandpa could hear as well.

Dani also, from where she was eavesdropping.

"You've rung Gianni but I can't answer at the moment. Please leave a message after the tone and I'll call you back."

Of course, Dad was on the plane, where you can't talk on your phone.

"Oh well," said Grandpa, giving up. "We'll say she can go then. It's sure to be all right."

He went to the kitchen to make a cup of tea.

Dani rushed over to Grandma.

"Thank you!" she puffed, and she
sank to the floor and hugged
Grandma's leg. "Oh Grandma,
you make everything all right."

Grandma nodded, pleased.

"Go and pack now, darling!" she said. "And put on something nice. Sonja said there would be a party!"

Then she went to the computer to buy tickets online.

Chapter 9

Dani changed at once into a dress she had been given as a present from Grandma. But the headband stayed on. It was so cool.

Then she hurried to pack her backpack with cards, drawing paper, felt pens and a few other things.

When that was finished she took her wheelie bag and put a little soft toy in it.

The hamsters watched her sadly.

They don't like it when she packs. It means she's going away, and sometimes they aren't allowed to go too.

"Don't be cross," said Dani. "I'm just going on a short trip to Northbrook to be a birthday present."

She stopped and thought a moment. It was fun to be an experience present, but Ella would probably like something else as well. She does really like things.

Imagine if Dani could put together a treasure hunt for her.

Treasure hunts are wonderful things to get!

This is what you do:

One person gathers up presents, wraps them in paper and lays them out so they make a trail. Then the other person has to go and look for them.

Dani hurried to get paper and string, which Grandma always kept in the kitchen drawers, and she started immediately.

First she took a glass bird and wrapped it in a piece
of paper with gold stars on it.

Then she took a teeny, tiny baby doll, which lay in a matchbox.

That had belonged to her mother.

In the third parcel, after some hesitation, she laid a ring with a blue stone—also her mother's, once upon a time.

"We give each other the things we love the most." She talked out loud to Ella. "The sort of things you'd never get from anyone else."

In the fourth parcel she wrapped a yellow rubber duck with sunglasses.

Ella collects rubber ducks.

In the fifth parcel she put a fan that Grandma had bought when she was in Spain.

In the sixth: a newly baked jam cake she had nipped from the kitchen and wrapped in greaseproof paper.

She cut out and wrapped and folded and taped and
made bows.

In the seventh parcel she wrapped a good book
that Grandma had just finished reading to her.
It was about a girl who was sold to a circus.

There wasn't much room for anything else besides a
toothbrush.

"What's all this?" Grandma wondered when she
came to check on her packing. "I thought *you* were
the present!"

"Yes, I am," said Dani. "The best present. But I
thought that Ella should have…"

"Yes, yes," Grandma interrupted, because she was in a hurry. "What about your nightie? And clean underwear? Sonja said you could stay for a few days!"

"I can borrow those things from Ella."

But Grandma packed some warm clothes anyway. "Now we'd better hurry," she said, taking out her hair rollers.

Dani said goodbye to the disappointed hamsters and gave them a pat.

"Up with the corners of your mouths! Soon you'll have me back again. You must understand, I've been longing for this for ages."

Then she took her phone, which was charging. Northbrook was waiting!

Chapter 10

And so, for the first time, Dani was venturing out in the world completely on her own. It felt enormous! Even bigger, almost, than the day she started school.

Going off on your own can be a bit scary the first time you do it.

How would she do?

Grandpa came running with his cup of coffee and he hugged her hard.

"Have a lovely time, Dani!" he said, trying to hide how worried he was. "It'll all go fine, just as I said."

And then Grandma drove her away.

Stockholm Central was crowded with people.

Dani took hold of Grandma so she wouldn't get lost in the rush.

First they went to the shop, where they bought a big banana and a magazine for Dani.

Then they found the right train and carriage and they stepped inside.

"This is your seat." Grandma pointed to a place by the window.

Dani was getting butterflies already.

"Don't talk to everyone you meet," Grandma said.

"But what if they talk to me?" asked Dani. "What shall I do then?"

"Pretend you can't hear them."

"Shall I pretend I'm deaf?"

"Yes, that's a good idea!"

The woman in the seat opposite looked interested.

"This little girl is going on her own to Northbrook," Grandma explained.

"I'm going there too," the woman said. "I can make sure she gets off at the right time. Will someone be there to meet her?"

"Of course," said Grandma. "A whole welcoming committee."

She hugged Dani, and Dani hugged her back. Several times. As if she didn't want to let go.

"You're allowed to change your mind," said Grandma. "Do you want to come home again to Grandpa?"

"No," said Dani. "I want you to come with me!"

"Sweetheart… What would happen to my bridge ladies then?"

"Forget about them!"

"Nonsense," said Grandma. "Everything will be fine. If you're worried about anything, you can always talk to this nice lady, or to the conductor."

Just then the man called the conductor came along and said that Grandma had to get off the train, because it was about to leave.

Grandma spoke briefly to him before she stepped down onto the platform.

That was the worst moment because the door closed at once and the train began to move.

Dani took a deep breath.

I'm coming, Ella, she thought. The best present is on its way. And a whole treasure hunt!

2

Chapter 11

The woman sitting opposite Dani looked at her curiously.

"Imagine your mother letting you travel so far on your own!" she said.

"My mother is dead," Dani replied.

"Oh, poor child!" cried the woman.

"And my father has gone to Rome," Dani continued.

The woman frowned. "That's hard for you."

"Yes," sighed Dani. It was quite hard.

"And your grandmother looks after you?" the woman went on.

"Only if she has time. Today she has to make dinner for her bridge ladies."

"Well I never!" said the woman. "That doesn't sound good. Do you often have to look after yourself?"

Dani remembered her promise to Grandma and she stopped talking. When the woman wanted to know more, she pretended not to hear.

They journeyed on in silence. After a while the woman took out a small paper bag.

"Would you like to try one?" she asked.

Now Dani could hear again. She nodded.

"Thank you," she said, and looked into the bag.

It was full of raspberry drops, licorice allsorts, jelly snakes and chocolates.

"How many am I allowed?"

"Three to start with," said the woman.

Dani took three raspberry drops and put them one
by one into her mouth. They tasted very good. She
looked expectantly at the bag.

But it stayed closed. The woman gave a huge yawn and put the bag in front of her on the little table.

And seconds later she was asleep.

That was a shame, but worse things can happen, Dani thought, and she looked out through the train window.

The sky was no longer holiday-blue. It had turned a heavy gray and, after a while, big flakes of snow came swirling down.

What did it matter though? Dani tried to calm herself. She was nice and warm, on a train that was rushing towards Northbrook, where a whole welcoming committee was waiting for her.

This is going really well, she thought. So far, in any case. But to be on the safe side she picked up her cell phone. She had to be ready if anything happened.

Chapter 12

It was a lovely phone that Dani had been given as a present from Sadie, Dad's girlfriend.

Dad didn't like the present. He doesn't think children should have cell phones. He's so stone-aged!

But Sadie had said that it could be useful and she'd put in three telephone numbers—one to him, one to Grandma and her own number. Then Dani had tried calling her while Sadie stood there.

Now she thought about doing it for real, but then she remembered something strange her father had let slip:

"I don't want you to call Sadie any more. I don't call her either."

"Is there something wrong?" Dani had asked.

"No…" Dad had answered, then immediately changed his mind. "Yes, you could say that."

And that was all he said.

But the strangest thing was that Sadie had moved. Not to the yellow house on Home Street, as they'd been talking about for a while. She had left Stockholm and moved to Northbrook—of all places in the world!

You could understand someone wanting to move there. Who wouldn't want to live in the same town as Ella?

But that isn't why Sadie settled there, Dad said. It's because she got a good job in Northbrook. And because her sister Lisette lives there. She's the one with Iceland ponies. And she's in the police! Who wouldn't want to live near a sister who's a police officer?

The weather grew wilder. Snow flurried down.

Dani peeled her banana and tried to read the magazine Grandma had bought for her.

But soon she let it drop. She sat and thought about what it would be like at Ella's party.

What games would they play? And what kind of cake would they have?

What if she made a little speech? Pinged on a glass, jumped up on a chair and said:

"I'm so glad you were born, Ella! And you too, Miranda Panda! And you, Ella's mother, and you, Extra Paddy! I'll celebrate you all as long as you live! And when you're dead too!"

Dani smiled, and about then she nodded off, just like the woman opposite.

She woke up to a voice on the loudspeaker.

"We will arrive shortly at Northbrook. The train will stop for two minutes. Two minutes!"

Dani shot up, threw her magazine into her backpack and poked the woman opposite.

"We've arrived!"

But the woman kept sleeping. Dani was about to poke her again, when the conductor came hurrying.

"Hello, miss!" he called. "Your grandmother said you're to get off here."

"She said she was getting off here too." Dani pointed at the woman.

The conductor didn't hear. "Come on, come on," he said, and he shuffled her in front of him, grabbing the suitcase on their way to the door.

Then he helped her down to the platform and
hopped back onto the train.

"The lady!" Dani persisted.

But the door closed, and the train slowly rolled
away.

Just as it gathered speed, Dani saw the woman
looking startled out the window.

Dani raised her hand and waved awkwardly before
looking around her in the snowstorm.

Where was the welcoming committee?

Chapter 13

The people who got off the train disappeared quickly, each to their own business.

Finally, Dani stood alone on the platform, looking around her.

Not a welcoming committee in sight!

What had happened? Had they forgotten?

She looked in all directions. She spun round ten times, twenty times, maybe thirty, and came at last to a standstill, staring straight ahead.

The whole station was covered in a thick white layer of snow and soon the cold began to creep into her body. It felt as if she were turning into an ice sculpture.

Eventually, a stationmaster appeared and began to clear the snow. When he caught sight of Dani he left it and came over to her.

"Are you waiting for someone?" he asked.

Dani nodded.

"Your mother?"

"No," shivered Dani, "sh…she's…d…dead."

"Is that so," said the stationmaster. "Well, who's coming instead of your mother, then?"

Dani gasped for air. Who was he talking about?

"Things take time in this sort of weather! Come with me to the station house before you freeze to death."

He took her suitcase and went off with it. Dani stumbled after him.

"You can stay here till she comes," he said as he opened the door to the waiting room.

"Who?"

"Like I said, whoever's coming instead of your mother."

Dani wanted to explain that she was waiting for a whole welcoming committee, but her lips were so numb she could hardly move them.

And soon he had disappeared back into the snowstorm.

Chapter 14

The waiting room was as dismal as the platform.

A sign had been put up on the counter of a little cafe over by the window.

Back soon, Dani read, and she sank down on a bench.

When she'd thawed out enough to move her fingers, she took out her phone again.

She had to talk to somebody.

But which of the three numbers should she choose?

Not Dad's. He'd be angry when he heard she was in Northbrook. She had that feeling.

And Grandma would have a heart attack if she knew that no one had come to meet Dani.

Then there was Sadie, who Dani wasn't allowed to phone.

I'll count to a hundred, she decided. If no one has come by then, I'll call anyway. One, two, three…

By the time she got to four she had pressed the number.

Sadie answered immediately.

"Hi Dani. I can't talk to you. I'm at work."

"I'm not allowed to talk either," said Dani quickly, "but I have to!"

"Where are you?"

"At the station!"

"Which station?"

"Northbrook! No one's come to get me…"

"Oh, you're in Northbrook!" cried Sadie.

Then someone told her to put away the phone.

"Stay right where you are," Sadie whispered. "I'll come and get you."

"When?"

"In an hour."

She might as well have said a year.

Dani felt a wave of panic.

"You have to come *now*!"

"It's not possible, but I'll try to get hold of my sister…"

The conversation ended. Dani swallowed her tears, put the phone on the bench and went over to the window to watch for Ella's mother.

But however hard she looked, she couldn't see Sonja's red car.

After a while she heard voices and turned around.

She wasn't alone in the waiting room any more.

At the door stood a pair of big boys watching her. They didn't look nice.

The big black dog with them didn't
look nice either. It could only see out
of one eye. The other eye was all white.

Suddenly Dani's phone rang.

Dani hurried over to the bench, but one of the boys got there first and picked it up.

"Hello," he said. "No, this isn't Dani. Goodbye!"

"Give me my phone!" cried Dani, trying to get it.

The dog barked, and Dani drew back.

"Pat Toto, and you can have it," said the boy.

When she reached for the phone again, the dog jumped up at her.

Dani was terrified.

"Take it away!" she shrieked, looking desperately around.

She backed away and scrambled under the bench, taking cover behind her suitcase.

Chapter 15

After that things happened very quickly.

The waiting room door opened. A woman in a purple coat rushed in and looked at a monitor with train times on it. Then she rushed out again.

The boys and the dog disappeared after her—with Dani's phone.

Dani stayed on the floor, afraid the dog would come back.

Then the door of the waiting room opened again, and she heard steps across the floor.

When she dared to look she saw big black shoes coming towards the bench.

They stopped, someone bent down, and a pair of eyes was staring at her.

It was Sadie's sister Lisette.

"Hello, it is you!"

Dani crawled out.

"What are you doing under the bench?"

Dani brushed herself off without answering.

"I called you," Lisette went on, "but a boy answered."

"Yes, he took my cell phone!" Dani muttered. "Him and his friend."

"What do you mean, took?"

Dani bit her lip.

"Did they take it here at the station?" Lisette persisted.

"Yes…"

"What did they look like?"

"Not very nice. They had a big black dog which jumped on me."

"Then I know who they are!"

Lisette took hold of Dani.

"Come on!" she said.

"Where are we going?"

"To get your phone back."

"In the police car?"

Anybody else who'd been robbed of their phone would say yes to an offer like that, but Dani resisted.

"I can't go," she said. "I have to wait."

"For Ella?"

"No, not for Ella. She mustn't know anything."

Lisette gave her a hard stare.

"Who exactly came with you?" she suddenly asked.

"I came by myself."

"You were on the train on your own?"

Dani nodded.

"And your father let you?"

"He's not allowed to know anything either!"

"But Dani!" said Lisette. "What's all this about?"

Dani tried hard to think what to reply.

"'A birthday present," she mumbled at last,
pointing to her headband.

She was close to tears.

When Lisette saw this, she decided to change her interrogation technique.

"How about a hot chocolate?" she asked, looking over to the cafe where the sign had disappeared. Someone was putting out plates of sandwiches and buns.

"I need a coffee," she added.

Chapter 16

The chocolate was good but hard to get down.
When Dani swallowed, her throat hurt. Still, she
forced herself to drink, because it warmed her up.

"Now you can tell me all about it," said Lisette.

"About what?" asked Dani.

"First of all, I'd like to know why you were hiding under the bench,"

Dani took another mouthful of the chocolate.

"It was that —— dog," she remembered with a bad word and a shudder.

"Goodness!" said Lisette. "Where did that little word come from?"

"From me!" said Dani, looking over to the window.

The red car was still nowhere to be seen. Instead she saw Sadie, half-running through the snow.

She wore a hat with a brim that almost covered her eyes.

Soon she was inside, shaking off the snow.

"Sadie!" Lisette sighed. "Must you wear that terrible hat?"

Sadie sank down on a chair.

"It's not a terrible hat. It's a slouch."

She smiled at Dani.

"A slouch?" said Dani. "Is that what it's called?"

"Yes, because it sort of slouches," Lisette explained.

"And not just the hat! My entire sister is slouching."

She turned to Sadie.

"Do you know that Dani came here completely on her own?"

Sadie took off her hat and Dani saw that her eyes were red from crying.

"Did your father send you?" she asked.

"No," answered Dani. "Dad mustn't know I'm here."

"Nor Ella either," added Lisette.

"But…why have you come, then?" Sadie wondered.

Dani swallowed and sank into a heap.

"I can't talk," she said. "I've got a sore throat."

"And a couple of our little thugs pinched her cell phone," Lisette continued.

Sadie, who had just taken a mouthful of her sister's coffee, almost spluttered.

"Do you have the number for Ella's mother?" Lisette asked.

Sadie took out her phone and called Sonja, but the ringtones sounded on and on.

"Why doesn't she answer?"

Sadie called again without result. Several times.

"What shall we do now?" she asked finally.

"The best thing would be to take Dani home again."

That brought Dani back to life.

"No!" she shrieked. "I've come to see Ella. Why didn't they come and get me? Sonja said they would."

"It could be the snow," said Sadie.

"You'll have to take care of this, sis," said Lisette. "I'm going to try and find Dani's cell phone."

She turned to Dani. "And you will go home! Do you hear what I say?"

Dani thought quickly.

"I'm too scared!" she said.

"What do you mean?"

"I don't dare go on my own."

"You managed all right getting here on your own."

"No, I didn't. But I did it anyway. I had to if I wanted to see Ella…"

"…who isn't allowed to know anything!" Lisette rolled her eyes and sighed. "This little girl needs a mother. Sadie, you'll have to go with her to Stockholm and make sure she gets home in one piece."

"I'll just have to do that, then," said Sadie, blowing her nose.

The sisters stood up.

"Come on, Dani, we'll go and buy the tickets," said Sadie.

Dani threw a last look out the window. There was no red car in sight, no cars at all any more.

"Come here, kid, for a hug," said Lisette.

Dani went reluctantly.

"I'm sure we'll meet again one day."

"Why shouldn't we?" Dani muttered.

"Dani doesn't know what's happened," said Sadie, putting her hat on again. "Or has Gianni explained it to you, Dani?"

"What? What don't I know?"

"A lot," said Lisette, tweaking her on the nose.

"Ouch!"

"Hurry up," said Lisette. "The train leaves in nine minutes."

Chapter 17

There was nothing Dani could do except obey.

"Come on, Dani," said Sadie.

But Dani did the opposite. She slowed her steps.

Dismayed and numb, she tore off the headband and threw it away. It was no longer needed.

Everything was ruined. All the surprises and the small presents. The whole trip!

And all the time the question buzzed in her head: Why hadn't the welcoming committee turned up?

Sadie stopped and held her hand out impatiently. Dani hesitated a little before she went and took it.

They struggled through the snow, which swirled around them. They got on the train without a word.

Dani sank into her seat and stared out through the window without seeing anything. At least not until she saw the train which had come in on the other side of the platform.

When the doors opened and the first passengers got out, something like an electric shock went through her.

Was she dreaming?

A girl who looked exactly like Ella jumped down onto the platform!

Suddenly her numbness vanished.

Ella, she thought. What are you doing here? Shouldn't you be at riding school?

After Ella came a girl who looked exactly like Miranda.

Why was *she* here too? Dani wondered.

She was supposed to be part of the welcoming committee!

Dani shot out of her seat and tried to open the window, but it was stuck.

"Ella!" she yelled, banging at the window.

But Ella didn't hear. She walked with her little sister towards someone waiting for them.

Someone who looked like their mother!

Dani's train started to move. There wasn't a second to lose! She had to get off, and get off fast.

Before Sadie could stop her, Dani ran back along the aisle and over to the door. She pulled the handle in panic, but the door wouldn't open. It was locked.

The train went faster. The platform slid away.

Dani fell to the floor and began to cry.

Sadie, who'd come after her, tried to calm her.

"Dani, listen to me," she said. "There must be some kind of misunderstanding."

But Dani didn't hear her.

"I want to go to Ella!" she cried.

"Please, Dani," said Sadie. "Crying won't help."

That was true. Nothing would help.

With a force that only a train possesses, Dani was being carried further and further away from the one person she wanted to be with all day, every day.

Always.

Chapter 18

She didn't stop crying until they reached the
next stop.

"Can we talk now?" asked Sadie.

"No, I have a sore throat," Dani reminded her.

"You're not getting sick?" Sadie felt Dani's forehead. "You're on fire! Dad will have to put you to bed when you get home."

"I'm not going home," Dani hiccupped.

"Yes, you are," said Sadie.

"I'm going to Grandma and Grandpa's! Dad's in Rome."

"In Rome? You're joking!"

"No, I'm not. He went this morning."

"And so he dumped you with Grandma and Grandpa?"

"He didn't dump me. Grandma came to get me in the car. I think he's sad…"

"I'm sad too!" Sadie cried. "Has he not said anything? Has he not told you that we've broken our engagement?"

Dani looked at Sadie, distraught.

"Were you *engaged*?"

"Yes, we were. Secretly."

"Were you planning to get *married*?"

"Yes. Would you have let us, little love?"

Dani hated being called little love and it wasn't the first time Sadie had done it.

She gave Sadie her irritated look.

"I'm sorry!" said Sadie. "I don't want to hurt you, but you haven't been exactly pleased about me…"

There were tears in Sadie's eyes.

She must have not wanted Dani to see because she took the hat from her knees and put it over Dani's head, so it covered the tip of her nose.

Dani swallowed and swallowed and tried to understand, then the hat was lifted again.

Then she leaned on Sadie's shoulder.

And Sadie put an arm around her.

They sat like that all the way to Stockholm.

3

Chapter 19

And so Dani went back to Grandma and Grandpa's house.

When they arrived, she felt so bad she couldn't even ring the doorbell, and Sadie had to.

Grandma came straight away and opened the door, in her best dress with her hair curled.

"But…what on earth…?" she cried.

"Dani is sick," said Sadie. "Can we come in?"

Then things got worse. Dani had hardly taken off her coat and gloves before Grandpa came with a thermometer.

Dani started to moan. She hated having her temperature taken.

"Come, Dani, let's go to your room," said Sadie, taking the thermometer. "Which one is yours?"

Grandpa showed her the way, and Sadie took Dani by the hand and shut the door.

Grandma and Grandpa stood outside, waiting for the wild scream that usually accompanied such occasions.

But this time they didn't hear a peep.

Soon Sadie looked out.

"This isn't good," she said. "It's pretty high. Do you have any children's medicine?"

Dani started to moan again. Medicine was another thing she hated.

"And I'll need a penlight," Sadie went on. "I need to look at her throat."

"No!" Dani cried.

But she needn't have, because just then the phone rang.

It was Dad, calling from Rome.

Chapter 20

Grandpa took the call.

"Can we talk in a minute?" he asked. "Dani's not well."

When Dad heard that he wanted to talk to her at once.

Dani took the phone and Dad's voice streamed into her ear.

"*Amore*, how are you?"

"Bad," Dani squeaked.

"Why haven't you called me?"

Dani tried to think. Why hadn't she?

Then she remembered:

"You would have been angry."

Dad flared up.

"How can you say that? I'm never angry with you! You must call me if there's something!"

Then Dani remembered something else.

"I didn't have my phone any more…"

"What did I say?" he snapped. "I knew you'd lose it! Children don't need cell phones!"

"I didn't lose it. Someone took it."

"What?"

Dani didn't want to explain any more, but Dad wouldn't give in.

"Where did that happen?"

"In Northbrook…"

"You're hallucinating!"

"No, I'm not. I was there."

"Have you been in Northbrook?"

"Yes."

"Who with? Grandma?"

"With myself."

When Dad realized that Dani had gone to Northbrook on her own, he went crazy.

"You know you can't do that! I can't trust you any more!" he shouted.

Dani swallowed. Ouch, it hurt.

"And I can't trust you either," she managed to say. "Why didn't you tell me that you and Sadie were going to get married?"

There was silence for a few seconds.

"Sadie?" Dad said then. "What's she got to do with this? Can I talk to Grandma?"

Grandma took the phone and began to talk loudly to Dani's father.

Dani held her ears and leaned against Sadie.

"Don't argue," she croaked.

But Grandma went on.

"You don't leave a sick little girl so you can run around in Rome!" she shouted. *"What sort of father are you, Gianni!"*

Dani crept under the covers and didn't come out again until Grandma had put down the phone.

"I don't know Gianni any more," she complained. "He should have said he'd be coming home this second!"

"Dani must have her medicine now," Sadie pointed out.

"Nooo," Dani wailed.

But no one was listening to her.

Grandma went to the kitchen and dissolved a pill in a glass of juice.

"Drink this, darling," she said.

Dani took a mouthful of the nasty medicine, but coughed it straight up and dropped the glass.

And all of it went in the bed.

Chapter 21

Right at that moment, a cheerful ringing on the doorbell announced that Grandma's bridge ladies had arrived.

Grandma became completely frozen.

What should she do? How could she look after them when Dani was so sick?

Grandpa went and opened the door. Immediately the small hall was filled with voices.

Grandma looked at Sadie, flustered.

"Off you go to your guests!" said Sadie. "I'll look after Dani."

She took Dani into the bathroom to wash her while Grandpa looked for a nightie and changed the bed.

Finally, Dani was tucked up in bed and Sadie went to get more medicine, the last bit Grandma had.

"You mustn't bring this one up," she said firmly. "Just swallow it and think of something fun!"

"What sort of thing?"

"Whatever you like best in the whole world!"

"Playing with Ella," said Dani weakly.

"Yes, of course. Think that: Ella, Ella, yes, yes, yes!"

Sadie popped the pill into Dani's mouth and held out a glass of water.

Dani drank it and thought of what Sadie had said. And the medicine slid down.

"That's the way! Soon you'll feel better," Sadie
promised.

"How much better?"

"So much that you'll want a sandwich with cheese
and tomato."

"And what will happen then?"

"We'll see."

"Will you get married then?"

Sadie looked astonished.

"Would you like that?"

"I want…"

Dani swallowed bravely.

"What do *you* want?" Sadie repeated.

Dani did the best she could: "I want Dad to be happy again."

Then she sank down in the bed and nodded off.

Chapter 22

After a while the murmurs and happy laughter from the other room woke Dani.

The bridge ladies were talking cheerfully, clinking glasses and cutlery, while Dani found it even harder to swallow.

She looked around. On a chair beside the bed sat Grandpa.

"Where's Sadie?" she croaked.

"Sadie went to the pharmacy to buy more medicine. Do you feel a little better?"

Dani shook her head and pointed to her throat. "Hurts!"

"Poor you! But listen to me, Dani. I forgot to tell you something. Gianni said that someone came to your house with a flower. Can you guess who it was for?"

"Me, of course," Dani said. "Who was it?"

"Oops, I forgot to ask!" said Grandpa.

"Maybe it was Cushion."

"Cushion?" laughed Grandpa. "Can that really be a name?"

"His name is Alexander," Dani managed to say. "But only when things get serious."

"And when would that be?"

"Grandpa, I can't talk any more!"

Dani pointed at her throat again.

To her relief, Sadie soon came back.

She felt Dani's forehead again.

"I'm dying," Dani gasped.

"Not at all," said Sadie. "But you need fluid. Maybe a little hot water and honey?"

Dani turned away. Honey water was one of the worst things she could think of.

"Think of something fun as you drink it up," Sadie ordered when Grandpa came back with the cup. But Dani couldn't think of any more things. Only one of her cousin Sven's jokes, which were never especially funny.

It went like this:

Why do some people eat snails?

Because they don't like fast food!

And Dani didn't like honey water! She put the pillow over her face and refused to drink.

But suddenly Sadie said something that made her ears prick up.

"I've talked to Lisette. She's managed to get your phone back."

Dani did nothing to show that she'd heard this good news.

"And I've talked to Sonja. Now I know why they didn't meet you at the station in Northbrook."

That made Dani lift the pillow.

"You came a day early," Sadie explained. "You and Grandma had the day wrong. Ella's birthday isn't till tomorrow."

Dani put the pillow over her head again.

She didn't drink any of the honey water.

4

Chapter 23

So that's how it was the time Dani would have been a birthday present but went on the wrong day. And got sick, very sick.

But luckily Sadie came and looked after her and sat by her bed for several hours.

"Sadie, are you still there?" Dani whispered each time she woke up from her feverish sleep.

"I'm still here," said Sadie.

"Don't go."

There was something Dani wanted to ask. But she could hardly talk any more.

Finally she managed.

"Do you think I need a mother?" she whispered.

"A mother?" Sadie was surprised.

"Yes…"

"Why would you need one?"

166

"To make sure I get to Northbrook on the right day," Dani croaked.

"Oh, of course," said Sadie. "That would be a good thing…"

Grandma says that Dani has a mother, even though she's not alive any more. She says you always have your mother.

You have her inside you, without thinking much about it. She's just there.

Dani didn't understand that when she was small, so then Grandma said that her mother had become an angel and was sitting on a cloud, waving.

When Dani was a little older and flew with Dad to Rome and saw the clouds up close through the plane window, she realized that it's not possible to sit on them.

Clouds are only thick fog. You'd fall straight through if you tried to.

Dani swallowed where she lay and peered at Sadie.

Finally Sadie got up and hugged Dani's foot, which was sticking out from under the covers.

"I have to go home now, anyway."

"No, wait!"

There was something else Dani wanted to know. But she couldn't talk any more. She could only whisper, croak or hiss.

"Would you be a stepmother if you and Dad got married?"

"No, never," Sadie cut her off. "Possibly a bonus mother, but now I won't be that either."

"I know," croaked Dani. "Because you've broken off the engagement."

"That's right," said Sadie. "Happy comes, happy goes…"

That reminded Dani.

"How does the rest of that poem go?"

Sadie thought.

"Where Dani goes, happy follows!" she said
finally.

"Do you mean as a birthday present?"

"No, I mean as a bonus child."

Sadie took out her handkerchief and blew her nose again.

Dani held out a hand to her.

"Are you sad too, Sadie?"

"Yes, very. It's awful, because now Gianni and I have to forget each other."

"No!" whispered Dani.

"Don't you understand?" said Sadie. "I've left him. I've even moved to Northbrook."

You can change your mind, Dani wanted to say. But she couldn't. She had no voice left.

Talk to Dad and tell him you don't have to forget each other just because one of you has moved to Northbrook, she wanted to say.

Don't be sad, she wanted to say. I'll make everything right again!

But she couldn't manage a single croak.

Sadie turned out the light and hovered in the doorway.

"Goodbye, Dani," she said. "Make sure Grandma and Grandpa give you medicine every five hours."
   Then she was gone.

Come back soon, Dani wanted to call after her.
   Don't forget me, she wanted to shout.

Chapter 24

Two more things happened that day. The first was that Ella called.

Grandpa came in with the phone.

"Are you awake?" he asked quietly.

"Mmmm," Dani managed.

"I'm sorry I wasn't home," Ella cried on the phone. "Miranda and I were with the Avocado in Linkoping!"

The Avocado is Ella's real father.

She has an extra father called Paddy, and she has her real father who she sometimes sees. He's a human rights advocate, but Ella always calls him Avocado.

"Can you hear me, Dani?" she continued.

"Mm-mm," mumbled Dani.

"What did you say? Speak properly! You're not dying, are you?" Ella sounded worried.

No, Dani wanted to say. Tomorrow I'm going to eat a cheese and tomato sandwich.

And I'm not going to die, she wanted to say.

Next time we're together I'm going to put on a treasure hunt for you, she wanted to say. Everything's already done.

But all she got out was another: "Mmmm."

Grandpa had to take the phone and explain.

But strangely enough Dani felt a little better after that. She only had to hear Ella's voice on the phone.

Or was it the medicine that had started working?

At last she noticed her hamsters, who were waiting for her to talk to them.

Didn't I tell you I'd be home soon, she wanted to say.

But her throat had completely stopped working.

Chapter 25

The second and final thing that happened that day was after the bridge ladies had gone home and there was peace and quiet in the house again.

Grandma and Grandpa had done the dishes and put everything away and were about to go to bed, when the doorbell rang.

There had never been so much ringing and clattering and racing about as there was in the house that evening.

"Probably one of your friends has forgotten something," said Grandpa, and he went to open the door.

But no, no! In the entrance stood Cushion with his red rose.

"I'm sorry to disturb you," he said, "but is there a girl called Dani living here?"

"There is," said Grandpa, "but she's asleep now. Are you the person called Alexander?"

"Yes, but only when things get serious." Cushion held out the rose.

All day he had worried that the expensive flower would die—but it was still alive.

Grandpa took the rose and sniffed it.

"It's very beautiful and it has a beautiful smell! But should you be out this late, young man?"

"My father couldn't bring me until now. He drives a bus."

"I see," said Grandpa. "I'll take the rose in to Dani so she sees it as soon as she wakes."

"Don't forget to tell her who it's from," said Cushion, before he ran out to his father, who was waiting on the street.

Grandpa put the rose in a vase of water and crept quietly in to Dani, who was properly asleep at last.

He put it on her bedside table and was about to sneak out again, when she opened her eyes.

"From Alexander," said Grandpa, pointing at the flower.

Dani nodded and closed her eyes again.

Alexander only when things are serious, she wanted to say. He's the one who wants to sit next to me in the classroom, where Ella's going to sit when she comes back.

But Cushion can sit there in the meantime of course…

"Happy comes, happy goes," echoed in her head, just the way her mother had said it.

"Where Dani goes, happy…" she'd continued.

No, wait! It was Sadie who added those words. But maybe Mama had said the same ones…

The rose nodded almost imperceptibly.

And Dani finally fell into a good, deep sleep.

Have you read the other books about Dani?

Dani is probably the happiest person she knows.
She's happy because she's going to start school.
She's been waiting to go to school her whole life.
Then things get even better—she meets Ella.

This is a story about Dani, who's always happy. She's unhappy too, now and then, but she doesn't count those times. But she does miss her best friend Ella, who moved to another town.

It's the second-to-last day of school and Dani's so happy she could write a book about it! In fact, that's exactly what she's done. But then she gets some bad news. How will she ever be happy again?

It's Dani's first summer break—her best one ever! Dani is staying on an island with Ella. They play all day long. They build huts, fish and spy on wild animals. They go swimming five, six, seven times a day.

Dani is on a school trip to the zoo when she gets lost. Then she sees someone she recognizes: Ella! Dani has to choose whether to follow her best friend in the world or follow the teacher's instructions.

This edition first published in 2019 by Gecko Press
PO Box 9335, Marion Square, Wellington 6141, New Zealand
info@geckopress.com

English-language edition © Gecko Press Ltd 2019

First published by Bonnier Carlsen, Stockholm, Sweden
Published in the English language by arrangement
with Bonnier Rights, Stockholm, Sweden
Original title: *Lycklig den som Dunne får*
Text © Rose Lagercrantz 2018
Illustrations © Eva Eriksson 2018

Translated by Julia Marshall
Edited by Penelope Todd
Typesetting by Katrina Duncan
Printed in China by Everbest Printing Co. Ltd,
an accredited ISO 14001 & FSC certified printer

Hardback (USA) ISBN: 978-1-776572-25-0
Paperback ISBN: 978-1-776572-26-7
Ebook available

For more curiously good books, visit geckopress.com